THE ADVENTURES OF

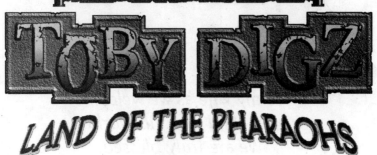

TOBY DIGZ

LAND OF THE PHARAOHS

By DAVID J. HERNANDEZ

Tommy NELSON®

www.tommynelson.com

A Division of Thomas Nelson, Inc.
www.ThomasNelson.com

*To my wife as we welcome
our child into this world.
We are truly blessed.*

Text & illustrations copyright © 2003 by David Hernandez

Published in Nashville, Tennessee, by Tommy Nelson®, a Division
of Thomas Nelson, Inc.

ISBN: 1-4003-0195-5

Printed in the United States of America

03 04 05 06 PHX 5 4 3 2 1

Contents

"We're set!"
Rosetta called
to Toby as she
and Lauren
stretched a rope
to make the
finish line.
Toby strapped
on his helmet and
cued his dog, "Okay,
Tut, hit it!"

Psssst . . . flip
the pages and
watch me climb!

Tut bolted forward pulling Toby on his skateboard. "Faster, Tut, faster!" Toby shouted. Tut lowered his head as his paws pounded the ground.

"Whoooaaaa! TOO fast!" Toby let go of Tut's leash and *zoomed* right past the finish line.

"Yea, Toby, yeaaaa!" cheered Rosetta.

Toby screeched to a stop and waved to the girls. Tut strutted up, wagging his tail. "Good boy!" Toby said as he scratched Tut's back. "That was the fastest we've ever gone!"

Just then, Charlie zipped up to join them. He stuck one foot out for everyone to admire his brand-new, jet-black, silver-trimmed, limited-edition skates. "I could beat you *and* your little puppy," Charlie boasted. "Dude, you're not *that* fast!"

EPOCH 2
The Race

"You think you're *sooo* cool," Rosetta said, pointing her finger at Charlie. "Toby could beat *you* any day!"

"Oh yeah?" Charlie sneered. "Then let's race! First one to the swings wins!"

"NOT a good idea! You could smack into a tree—or each other!" Lauren warned.

"That's okay," Charlie snickered, walking away. "I knew Toby was chicken anyway."

Rosetta stood on her toes to face Charlie. "Toby Digz is NOT CHICKEN!" She turned to look at Toby. "Right, Toby? You'll race him, won't you, Toby?"

"Uh, yeah, sure," Toby agreed. "I'll race."

Toby and Charlie were perched on the starting line.

Lauren announced, "Oooon your mark, geeet set, GO!"

And they were off! Charlie sprang into action and began weaving wildly through the trees, while Tut shifted Toby into high gear. When Tut saw Charlie beside him, he leaped forward, pulling Toby into the lead.

"WOOF!" Tut barked.

"We're doing it, Tut. We're going to win!" Toby called. But, just then—"Left, Tut, LEEEEFT!!"—Toby noticed a large root jutting up from beside an oncoming tree.

It was too late.

Toby's skateboard bounced over the root, sending him flipping and flying over Tut to land headfirst in the sandbox. Tut slid in right behind him, sending a wave of sand over Toby's head.

EPOCH 3
A Sandy Sphinx

"Well, I guess this means I won!" Charlie gloated, inspecting his new skates for scratches. "You look like that statue thing in **Egypt**!" he laughed, as Toby's head popped out of the sand.

"It is *called* the Great **Sphinx**," Toby corrected.

Lauren and Rosetta ran to the sandbox. "Are you okay?" Lauren asked, pulling Toby out of the sand.

"What are 'gray finks'?" Rosetta asked.

"The Sphinx is—*puh!*—way cool!" Toby said, spitting sand from his mouth. "It's this huge statue in Egypt that sits in front of the **pyramids** like a giant guard dog."

"*Aliens* built the pyramids," Charlie said.

"Oh, Charles!" Lauren rolled her eyes. "That's ridiculous!"

"How do you know all that stuff about Egypt, nerd?" Charlie demanded.

"See for yourself," Toby answered. "To the tree house!"

Rosetta looked up at Lauren and smiled. "To the tree house!" they both cheered.

"What's the big deal with the tree house?" Charlie asked.

"You'll see," Toby said.

"Didn't you know?? Toby is going to be an **archaeologist**," Rosetta gushed, "and his Uncle Abe runs the museum and he gave him all this awesome stuff, like an **Epoch Clock** and scrolls and . . ."

"Come on, Rosy," Lauren interrupted. "He'll find out for himself."

EPOCH 4

To the Tree House!

Charlie was the last one up the ladder. "Whooa, cool!" he shouted when he reached the top. "Uh, I mean, this place is okay," he added quickly.

Lauren pulled Tut up on the **Doggy-vator** as Toby looked through the old scrolls.

Toby read:

The first Hebrews who moved to Egypt found favor in the eyes of the Pharaoh. But generations later, a Pharaoh came to power who enslaved the Hebrews. Until one day . . .

"What, Toby?!?" Rosetta squealed. "What happened next?!"

"Wait, why did God even let them be slaves?" asked Charlie.

"Maybe we'll find out," answered Toby, checking his **Jampak** for all the gear. "Don't forget your charts and maps this time," Lauren teased.

Toby shoved a bunch of papers into his pack and led the others into his imaginary cave of blankets and boxes.

"What is all of this junk?!" Charlie asked, ducking through the blankets.

"You'll see." Toby instructed, "You have to close your eyes and use your imagination . . . IF you want to know more."

"C'mon, boy!" Toby called to Tut.

"Hurry up!" Charlie insisted.

"Oh, Charles. There's *nothing* to be afraid of," Lauren told him.

"Who said I was afraid?" Charlie snapped. "I just don't like being in the dark with a bunch of kooks!"

"Sure," Lauren replied over Rosetta's giggles.

Just then Toby shouted:

"LET'S DIG INTO THE BIBLE!"

They crawled through the dark cave and out into the bright, midday sun. Toby shielded his eyes. "This is my Epoch Clock," he told the others. "It tells us exactly where we are."

"Then . . . where are we??" Charlie asked, looking around.

"We're in ancient Egypt," Toby replied. "The Land of the **Pharaohs!**"

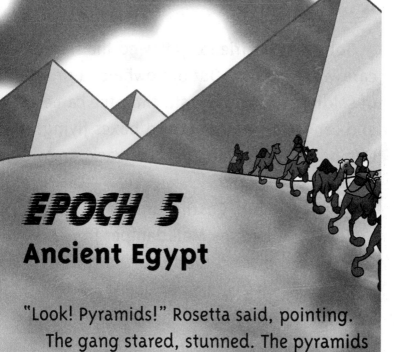

EPOCH 5
Ancient Egypt

"Look! Pyramids!" Rosetta said, pointing.

The gang stared, stunned. The pyramids stood like giants on the horizon.

Toby tried to focus on some blurry figures on top of the hill. "Check it out!" he yelled as he and Tut took off toward them. "It looks like they're taking things into the city to trade with the Egyptians. C'mon!"

Toby and his friends followed the sandy caravan into town. Out of nowhere, a group of soldiers charged by, startling the camels and sending the baskets and boxes flying! One box hit the ground with a crack, and—

SSSSSSSS—

"SSNAAAKESS!" Charlie jumped back.

Toby grabbed the **Metadamper** from his Jampak and blasted the snakes with water.

"Whew!" Charlie gasped as the snakes slithered away.

"TOOOBY!!!" Rosetta was unable to move, staring at the chariot heading straight for her.

Activating his **Dashpads**, Toby sprang out over the street. He grabbed Rosetta as the chariot raced by.

"Oh, my heeero!" Rosetta batted her eyelashes at Toby.

Toby blushed. "Let's get out of here before someone ELSE gets in trouble!"

EPOCH 6
The Great Sphinx

"Look! The **Nile**!" Toby pointed ahead. "It's the longest river in the world."

"The Nile," Lauren began, "that's where the Pharaoh's daughter found baby Moses!"

"Yeah," agreed Toby, "then Moses grew up to free the Hebrew people from slavery."

"How did he do that?" Charlie asked.

"I think we're going to find out," answered Toby.

As they walked along the Nile, snakes slyly slid into the water. Lauren held a nearby tree limb for balance as she peered into the river.

Crraaaaack!

The limb gave way, and Lauren tumbled into the murky water. "HEEeeeelllp!" she screamed, as the current pulled her away from the shore.

Toby tossed his Jampak to Charlie and yelled, "Find my **Ripkord** and wait for my signal!"

Charlie dug through the Jampak as Toby swam toward Lauren. The water rolled off a curious crocodile as he raised his head to study the intruders.

"OH, NO!" Rosetta screamed, jumping up and down on the riverbank. "Oh, no! Oh, no! Oh, no!" She noticed the large eyes—and even larger teeth—swimming closer to Lauren.

"Now!" Toby yelled. Charlie threw the Ripkord straight into Toby's outstretched hand. Toby reached for Lauren and cast the Ripkord at a nearby tree trunk.

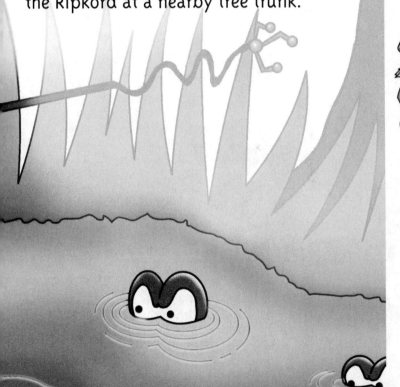

Toby was struggling against the current to pull Lauren in, when she was—somehow—raised out of the water by a huge hippopotamus!

"Aaa-ruff ruff!" Tut barked, and the hippo responded by bringing Lauren to shore. She stepped off, relieved to have solid ground under her feet again.

"Ruff woof!" Tut barked to the hippo as it sank back into the river.

"I think I've seen enough of the Nile," Lauren told Toby with a sheepish grin.

"Right." Toby smiled. "Let's see what else we can find . . ."

After what seemed like forever, they saw a large figure in the distance. "Come on! It's the Sphinx!" Charlie yelled, running for it.

They all looked to see the head of the giant statue over the hill. Toby and the girls ran, trying to keep up with Charlie.

"We're neeever going to get there," Rosetta whined, as their running slowed to walking again.

The sun was going down when they finally reached the Sphinx. "WHOAA! It's HUGE!!" Charlie climbed onto one arm of the Sphinx. "Can we go inside?"

"I don't know," Toby answered. "Some people think there's a big chamber inside, but no one knows for sure."

"I'm going to be the one who finds out!" declared Charlie.

"Oh great," Lauren moaned.

EPOCH 7
A Secret Passageway

"I'll beat you to the top!" Charlie called as he scrambled higher and higher up the Sphinx.

Lauren shook her head. "Everything is a race to that boy."

"How tall is the Finks, anyway?" Rosetta asked.

"Let's see," Toby said grinning. Tut held Toby's Jampak while Toby pulled out a scroll. "The Great Sphinx is 240 feet long and 66 feet high. It appears to be a lion's body with the head of a man, but no one knows whose face it has."

Charlie climbed higher and higher. He called down to the others, "Look at me!"

"You could get stuck up there!" Lauren shouted.

"He better not!" Toby said. "I'm not going up there after him!"

"I . . . I . . . made it," Charlie panted. He leaned on the tip of the statue's crown and waved at the others. Suddenly, something behind him moved, and Charlie began to fall down, down, down into darkness. "Mommmmyyy!!" he cried as he disappeared into the Sphinx.

"Looks like he found a secret passage!"
Lauren cried.

"And now we have to find *him*,"
Toby grumbled. "Tut, let's look for
another way in." Tut began to sniff
around the base of the Sphinx.
The moon was rising, and it
was getting very dark.

EPOCH 8

In the Belly of the Sphinx

"RRRrrrrrrrrrrrr . . ." Tut was growling on the other side of the Sphinx.

Toby found him clawing at a stone that was a bit out of place. "Good work, boy! You scouted out a doorway."

Toby reached into his Jampak, pulled out a small shovel, and began to dig around the stone. Tut helped Toby dig.

"One, two, three—PULL!" Lauren called as they all tugged at the large stone. And with that, it sprung loose, scattering a cloud of dust around them.

Toby peered down into the dark chamber. "Can't see a thing!" He clicked on his flashlight. "Charlie? You down there?" But there was no answer.

Toby pulled out a long rope and gave it to Tut. Tut held the rope tightly while Toby lowered himself into the pitch black below.

After a few minutes, Toby yelled up to the girls. "It's okay. C'mon down."

Lauren and Rosetta climbed down after him. Then Tut dove down into Toby's arms.

Darkness surrounded them. "I'm sc . . . sc . . . scared," Rosetta whispered.

"Me, too, but God is looking out for us," Toby said calmly.

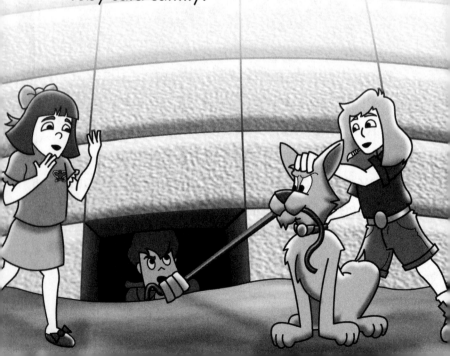

They began to search the eerie passages, inching sloooowly around corners, and calling for Charlie.

As they turned one especially dark corner, Toby spotted something especially tall and looming.

"AAAHHH!!" Lauren and Rosetta screamed in unison.

"Look! It's just old statues," Toby said as he got close enough to see.

As they tiptoed up a winding staircase, Rosetta looked up and whispered, "God, *puh-lease* help us find Charlie." But just then, the stairs began to crumble beneath their feet.

"It's a booby-traaaa—" Toby yelled as he fell.

They all jumped quickly
to their feet. Toby looked
around, just in time to see a
hand reach out of the darkness
and grab Lauren's arm.

"AAGGHH!"

"HA! It's just me," Charlie said. "There's *nothing* to be afraid of," he mocked.

"Oh, I'm so glad to see you," Lauren sighed. "But I'm still mad!"

Charlie was pretty happy to see them, too.

Rosetta looked up again. "Thank you."

EPOCH 9
I Want My Mummy!

"We have *got* to find a way out of here," Toby told them, "and quick, before the Pharaoh's soldiers discover the way *in*."

"Hey, follow me!" Charlie said as he led them into a crowded room. "I think we can climb out."

"Why do you think the Egyptians built so many of these things?" Lauren asked, pointing to the corner of the room.

Toby shone his flashlight on the face of a tall, golden statue. "That's a **sarcophagus**," he said, "an old mummy case—like a coffin. There are some of these in my uncle's museum."

"M-mummy case? As in *dead* people?" Charlie whimpered. "We've GOT to get out of here!"

"*You* said we could climb out," Lauren reminded him.

"I thought it was this room." Charlie felt along the wall for another doorway. "Ooo, I found something," he said, pulling on a small lever. Another trap!

Hidden doors opened upward out of the floor and raised the mummy cases.

Crreeeaaaakkkk!

Toby spun around with his flashlight to see the old coffins swinging open and crumbling mummies falling toward them.

"Aaaaahhhh! They're after us!" Charlie yelled.

"MUMMIES!" they screamed, scattering in all directions.

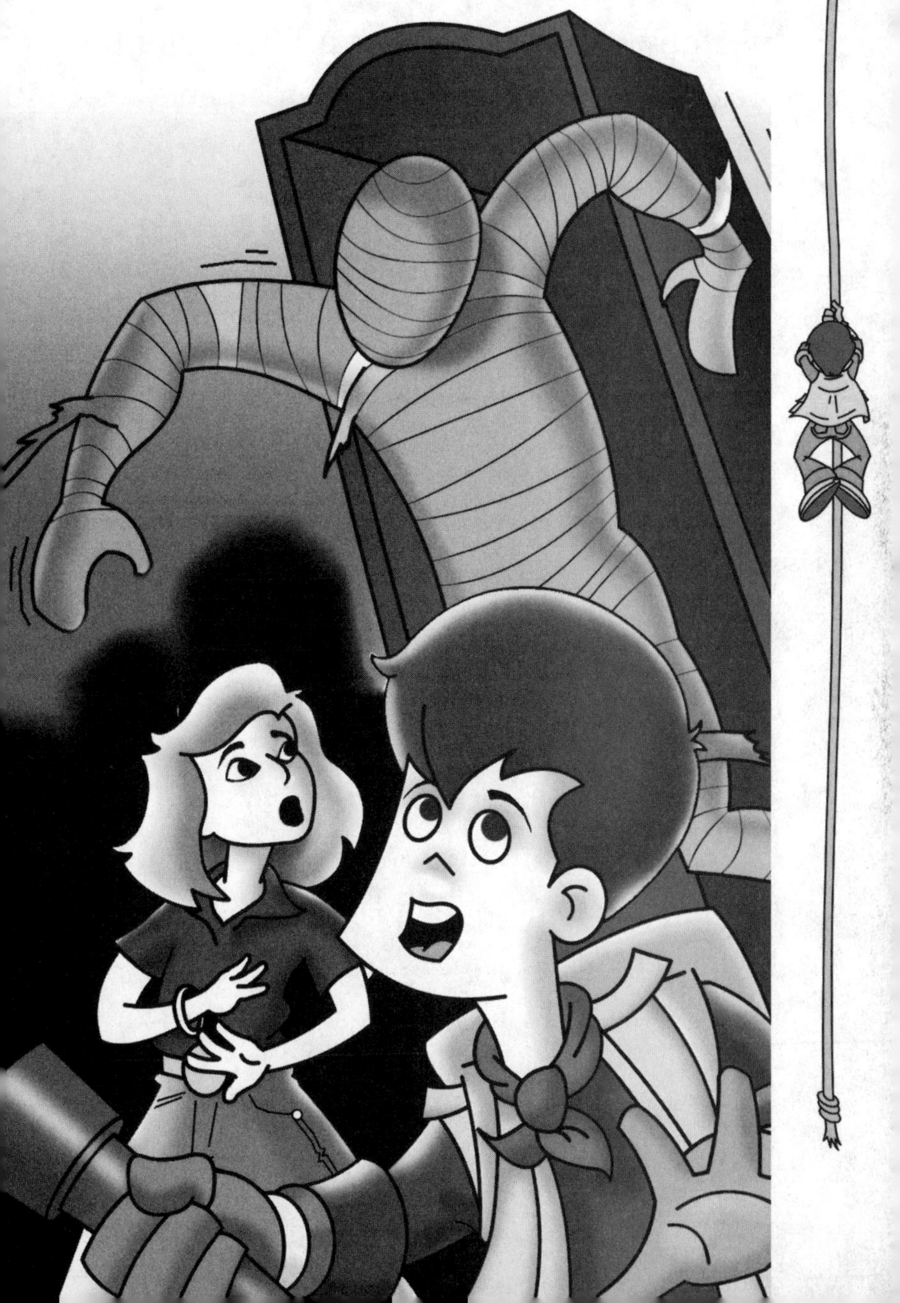

EPOCH 10
The Glowing, Green Eyes

"ARRROOF!" Tut barked loudly, and the gang rushed toward him. He had found a way out.

Charlie pushed past Toby, bumping his arm and sending the flashlight flying into a deep, black hole. Toby stared at his empty hand in disbelief. As the gang entered the room, the four of them peered into total darkness.

"Uhh . . . who is *that*?" Charlie asked.

"I'm right beside you," Toby answered.

"Rosetta and I are over here," Lauren whispered.

"Then who . . . who are *they*?" Charlie winced.

They all swung around and saw hundreds of glowing, green eyes. Rosetta ran screaming in the other direction.

Charlie darted as fast as he could. "AHHHHHHH!!!" he and Lauren screamed as they smacked into one another.

"This way!" Toby called as he and Tut tore off down a passageway toward another room.

"How many rooms *are* there?" Rosetta panted.

But it was too late. The glowing eyes were right behind them. The eyes inched closer, closer, CLOSER!

"Mmmeow." One tiny kitten walked out from the shadows.

"AGGGGHH!" Charlie leaped into Lauren's arms.

"Aww, it's just a widdle kitty," Rosetta laughed.

"Oh, yeah! The Egyptians raised thousands of cats," Lauren said. "I bet they're everywhere!"

"*I* even knew that," Rosetta added.

Charlie jumped out of
Lauren's arms. "I-I knew that too,"
he said. "I was just protecting *you*
in case . . . in case it was more mummies."

"Right," Lauren smirked.

"Look up there," Toby said pointing.
"Light is shining through. If we can
get up there, maybe we can
climb out."

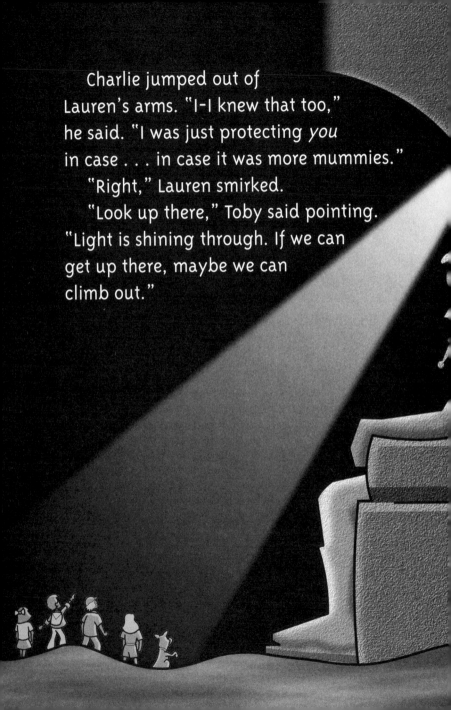

EPOCH 11

A Narrow Escape

One at a time, the gang began to climb out of the Sphinx. Lauren went first, then helped Rosetta out.

"AHH! Fresh air!" Rosetta took a deep breath as she climbed through the opening.

"Me next!" Charlie insisted.

As Lauren pulled him into the sunlight, she noticed something on top of his head—something black . . . and fuzzy . . . with eight legs.

"Eeek!!!! SPIDER!" she screamed, letting go of Charlie's hand.

Charlie fell back into the hole, toppling Toby and Tut. "Where is it?! Where IS it?!?" He jumped up, flailing and swiping at his head. "Yuck!" Charlie shivered as the spider scurried away.

After regaining his cool, Charlie reached again for Lauren. She helped him out and helped to brush the dust from his clothes.

"Sorry for letting go," Lauren said. "I didn't—"

"It's okay," Charlie interrupted, smiling.

Toby climbed out and lowered a rope to pull up Tut. "We made it!" Toby said.

"See what a little teamwork can do?" Lauren said, winking at Charlie.

"Okay," Toby began, "first let's rest, and then we'll check out those pyramids." He looked at Charlie. "And, please, nobody do anything daring for awhile."

EPOCH 12
Pyramids 101

By this time, the moon was shining high in the sky. Tut stood guard while the others rested.

"Why did the Egyptians draw on *everything*?" Rosetta asked.

"That's Egyptian writing," Toby said with a laugh. "Each character is called a **hieroglyph**. The Egyptians recorded their history that way."

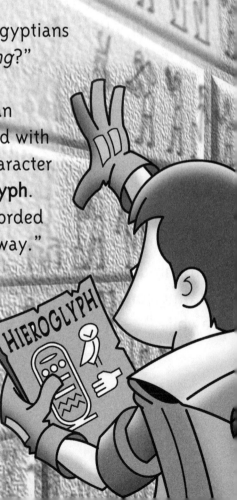

"All right, let's go!"
Toby said after a short rest,
and he led the way to the
Great Pyramid.

The closer they got, the harder it
was for them to see all the way to the
top of the pyramid. Finally, they just
stopped and stared. It was huge!

"Did you know," Toby began, "if
we were to lay all of the stones from
the Great Pyramid in a straight line,
they would reach across the United
States and back?"

"Whooaaahh!" Charlie exclaimed.
Toby just smiled.

EPOCH 13

A Dusty, Old Man

The foursome turned to make the long walk back toward the city. As they approached the city, Tut began to bark wildly at something behind them.

They slowly turned around and found themselves face-to-face with a dusty, old camel. And on top of that dusty, old camel sat a dusty, old man.

"Oh boy." Charlie gulped. "What now?"

As the man slowly passed, he warned them in a deep voice, "Children, these streets will soon be unsafe. You should go home. God be with you." The old man waved and continued into the city.

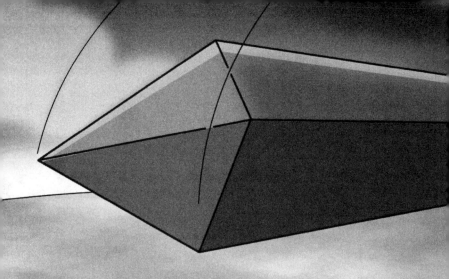

"That was kind of spooky," Rosetta whispered.

"You know . . . I think that was Moses— on his way to free the Hebrew people!" Toby shouted as he realized who they'd just met. "He's probably headed for the Pharaoh right now! Come on!"

On their way to the Pharaoh's palace, the gang stopped to take a short break. Rosetta leaned on a . . .

"Rosetta, watch out!!!" Toby yelled.

"Ooops," Rosetta peeped, "what is that?"

"That *was* an ancient **obelisk**," Lauren said.

"The Egyptians are really proud of their obelisks," Toby explained. "Each one is carved out of a single piece of stone and brought down the river. They had to drag that stone a long way to get it here."

"And here they come now!" Lauren pointed at the soldiers coming toward them.

"Arrest them!" one soldier ordered. "They have broken the Queen's obelisk!"

Rosetta just stood staring at the rubble. Toby grabbed her by the hand and ran.

Lauren and Charlie followed close behind. Tut tried to trip up the soldiers while the gang found a place to hide.

"I think we lost them," Toby whispered with a sigh of relief.

After catching her breath, Lauren jumped up. "Hey! We're going to miss Moses and the Pharaoh!"

Tut rejoined the gang as they snuck into the Pharaoh's grand palace. There they saw the Pharaoh draped in shimmering gold, surrounded by guards.

"We got here just in time," Toby whispered to the others.

They watched quietly as Moses approached the Pharaoh. "Let my people go," he said. But the Pharaoh just laughed and sent Moses away.

"He's mean!" Rosetta shouted.

"Shhhh!!!" the others said, all reaching to cover her mouth.

They watched as Moses left the palace.

Lauren shook her head. "Oh no, you know what *this* means . . ."

EPOCH 14

Frogs & Flies & Locusts, Oh My!

"What?! What *does* this mean?!" Rosetta asked.

"Well, God wanted Moses' people to be free, too. And since the Pharaoh won't free them, God is going to send down **plagues** on Egypt," Toby answered.

"Uhh, w-what kind of p-p-plagues?" Charlie stammered.

"Come on. Let's go," Toby said, leading them out of the palace.

When they got outside, people were running through the streets screaming. "The river! It's red!" one woman cried in disbelief.

"Oh no! The plagues have already started!" Toby shouted. "If we close our eyes and concentrate, we can imagine ourselves into the future—the same way we got here!"

So they imagined into the future—but not quite far enough.

Suddenly, millions of slimy, green frogs hopped onto the land. Charlie shouted, "Let's get out of heeeere!"

"Ew! Ew! Get these slimy things off me!" Rosetta cried as a midair frog splatted against her leg.

"Aroof!" Tut barked as he scrambled onto some nearby crates.

"Quick! Let's try it again," Toby yelled. They tried to imagine themselves farther into the future.

Charlie opened one eye. "Is it over?"

"Looks okay to me," Lauren replied.

"Whew! I don't care if I ever see another frog again!!" Rosetta cried.

Suddenly, the sky over Egypt turned smoky gray.

"It's getting really dark," Rosetta whispered.

"Grrrrrr . . ." Tut growled.

Toby looked off into the black sky. "Oh, no! It's the plague of darkness! We have to get out of here . . . NOW!"

They tried it once more: closed their eyes tight and imagined . . .

EPOCH 15
The Big Party

When they opened their eyes, the sky was bright again. Toby and his friends ran to a nearby house for safety.

Lauren knocked on the door. "Ooh, you know what that is?" she asked, noticing a red stain above it. "They're marking their doors to protect their sons! We learned in Bible class that with the last plague, the oldest son in every Egyptian family was to die. BUT God told Moses that if the Hebrews marked their doors, their boys would be safe."

The door swung open. "Please, come inside," a man said. The gang entered and looked around. The man's family was singing and laughing and eating. The man gave bread to Toby and his friends.

"Here, Tut," Charlie whispered, feeding Tut his bread.

"What's going on?" Rosetta asked, listening to the cheers outside.

"The Hebrew people are happy because they get to leave," Toby whispered.

"Arrooff!" Tut scratched at the door and wagged his tail.

"Oh, okay," the Hebrew man laughed and let Tut back outside.

Outside, the Hebrews were all laughing and dancing. It was one HUGE party! Rosetta and Lauren giggled and danced through the door and out into the crowd. Toby and Charlie followed, while Tut skipped along beside them.

"The Hebrew people are free!" Toby said, spotting Moses on a nearby hill.

"Today, after four hundred years of bondage," Moses began saying to the people below, "our people are free to leave Egypt!"

"At last! At last!!" the people shouted.

"Well, I guess those plagues did the trick!" Charlie said.

"Yup," Toby said. "In the last plague, the Pharaoh lost his own son. He was so upset that he finally gave in and said the Hebrews could leave."

Back to the Tree House!

"Look! Tut found the cave!" shouted Lauren.

"Well, at least we got to see the **Exodus** before leaving," Toby sighed.

"We need to 'exit us,'" Rosetta said. "My mom's going to be looking for me."

"Aroof!" Tut barked and they all entered the cave—their ticket home.

They crawled through the darkness until they felt the familiar wooden planks of the tree house floor.

"Wow, that was awesome!" Charlie said.

"Now you see why I like to learn so much about Egypt," Toby said.

"That was toooo cool!" Lauren said, still dancing.

"Wait . . . I just have one more question," Charlie said. "Why did God make the Hebrews wait so long as slaves in Egypt?"

"Ooo! Oo! I know!" Rosetta cried, waving her hand in the air. "Sometimes, we want God to help us right now, but God *always* knows the best time for everything!"

Toby and Lauren exchanged glances and smiled at Rosetta.

"Yeah. That makes sense," Charlie said. "But, speaking of time, I've GOT to get home."

"See you later alligator!" Toby called to him.

"On the NILE crocodile!" Charlie called back and laughed.

The End

THE PYRAMID

INSIDE THE GREAT PYRAMID OF KHUFU

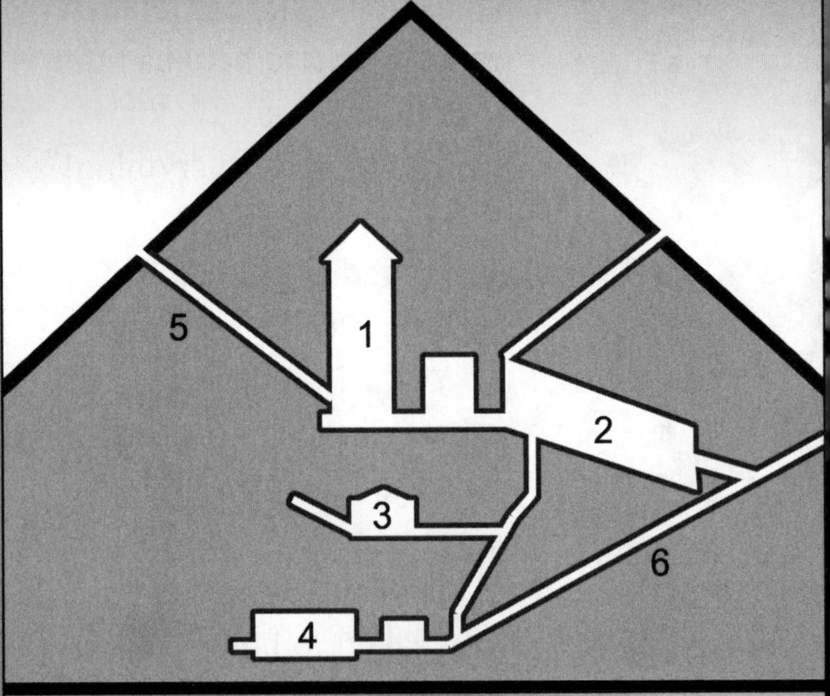

1 - KING'S CHAMBER
2 - GRAND GALLERY
3 - UNFINISHED CHAMBER
4 - ORIGINAL CHAMBER
5 - HALLWAY TO STARS
6 - ENTRANCE SHAFT

DIGZIG

TOBY'S SECRET PICTURE WRITING

Toby made up his own picture writing just like the hieroglyphs the Egyptians used. Use this page to translate the secret messages Toby has hidden in this book!

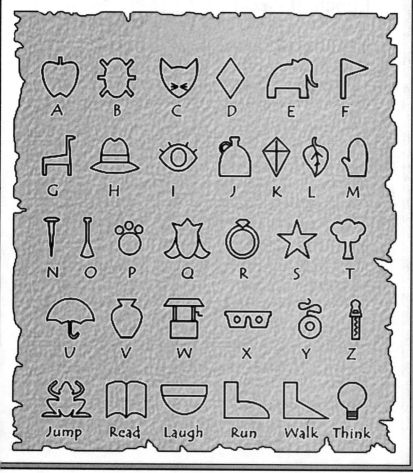

A B C D E F

G H I J K L M

N O P Q R S T

U V W X Y Z

Jump Read Laugh Run Walk Think

DIGZ-TIONARY

Archaeologist (ar-kee-OL-uh-jist)
a person who learns about history by digging in the ground and studying the items found

Egypt (EE-jipt)
a country in northern Africa

Epoch (EE-pok)
a period of time marked by certain events

Exodus (EX-uh-dus)
the Hebrew escape from Egypt, led by Moses

Hieroglyph (HI-er-o-gliff)
picture writing used by the Egyptians

Khufu (KOO-foo)
the king of Egypt around 4,500 years ago

Nile (nyle)
the long river that flows through Africa

Obelisk (OB-uh-lisk)
a very tall and skinny pyramid-style tower

Pharaoh (FAIR-o)
the Egyptian word for *king*

Plague (playg)
a disaster or disease affecting lots of people at once

Pyramid (PEER-ah-mid)
a giant triangle-shaped building in Egypt

Sarcophagus (sar-KOF-uh-gus)
a Pharaoh's coffin box made of stone

Sphinx (sfinks)
a very old statue in Egypt with the head of a man and the body of a lion

DIGZ GEAR

JAMPAK
Toby's backpack

METADAMPER
water-spraying device

DASHPADS
high-flying jump boots

EPOCH CLOCK
time and space sensor

RIPKORD & ZIPCLIP
safety cable and reel

DOGGY-VATOR
Tut's tree house elevator

Check out all of the DigzGear online at www.tobydigz.com

LET'S DRAW
TOBY DIGZ

1

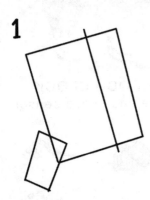

Draw these squares.

2

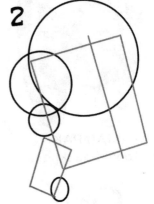

Now draw these circles.

3

Next, draw the eye circles, mouth triangle, and the hair lines.

4

Then finish up the drawing.

KEEP PRACTICING!

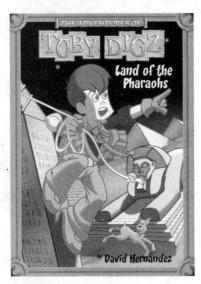